Backyard SPORTS

Home Field Advantage

By Michael Teitelbaum

Illustrated by Ron Zalme

Grosset & Dunlap • A Stonesong Press Book

A Stonesong Press Book

GROSSET & DUNLAP
Published by the Penguin Group
Penguin Group (USA) Inc., 375 Hudson Street, New York, New York 10014, USA
Penguin Group (Canada), 90 Eglinton Avenue East, Suite 700,
Toronto, Ontario M4P 2Y3, Canada
(a division of Pearson Penguin Canada Inc.)
Penguin Books Ltd., 80 Strand, London WC2R 0RL, England
Penguin Group Ireland, 25 St. Stephen's Green, Dublin 2, Ireland
(a division of Penguin Books Ltd.)
Penguin Group (Australia), 250 Camberwell Road, Camberwell,
Victoria 3124, Australia
(a division of Pearson Australia Group Pty. Ltd.)
Penguin Books India Pvt. Ltd., 11 Community Centre, Panchsheel Park,
New Delhi—110 017, India
Penguin Group (NZ), 67 Apollo Drive, Rosedale, North Shore 0632,
New Zealand (a division of Pearson New Zealand Ltd.)
Penguin Books (South Africa) (Pty.) Ltd., 24 Sturdee Avenue,
Rosebank, Johannesburg 2196, South Africa

Penguin Books Ltd., Registered Offices: 80 Strand, London WC2R 0RL, England

Library of Congress Control Number: 2008006778

ISBN 978-0-448-44899-2   10 9 8 7 6 5

Chapter One

"I'm open, Achmed!" Joey MacAdoo shouted to his teammate as he raced along the sideline. "Pass it here!"

Achmed Khan dribbled the soccer ball, softly tapping it from foot to foot. He was trying to keep the ball away from Ramon Hardison, who was guarding him closely.

Achmed and Joey's team, the Lightning, were playing against their biggest rivals, Ramon and his fellow Flyers. The two teams competed in every sport, but the action was especially intense on the soccer field. With just under five minutes left in the second half, the Lightning trailed 3–1.

Achmed stopped, trapping the ball with the bottom of his foot to bring it to a stop. Ramon tried to slow down, but his momentum carried him past Achmed.

That was all the space Achmed needed. He planted his left foot and fired a rocket pass to Joey with his right.

Joey streaked toward the Flyers' goal. He had one player to beat, Andy Turner. Andy was the Flyers' speedy sweeper. He reached the ball at the same moment as Joey.

"That's yours, Andy!" shouted Amanda Wilson, the Flyers' goalie. She set herself in front of the goal.

As Andy reached for the ball with his right foot, Joey tapped it with his left—in the opposite direction from the one in which he was running. The ball sped back past both of them. Joey stopped quickly and changed direction. Andy reacted quickly, too, but he was a step behind Joey. Joey caught up to the ball at the corner of the Flyers' penalty area.

Amanda hurried across the goal to line herself up for Joey's shot.

Seeing this, Joey twisted his body slightly and slammed the ball with his right foot—aiming for the far-left corner of the goal.

Amanda dove, stretching her body out and reaching out with her left hand. The ball grazed her fingertips, slammed into the left goalpost, and rolled into the goal.

"Score!" shouted Vicki Kawaguchi, Joey's teammate.

Joey's goal had cut the Flyers' lead to 3–2 with four minutes left in the second half.

"Killer shot, Joey!" Achmed yelled to his teammate. "Now let's tie this thing up!"

"Not likely!" Ramon shouted back.

Joey placed the ball right in the middle of the center circle, then skipped backward into his team's territory.

Once the two teams had set up on either side of the center line, the Flyers' striker kicked the ball to put it back in play. He sent a pass bounding to teammate Justin Martell, who hurried down the left sideline.

Ramon raced down the center of the field toward the Lightning's goal. He spun past Joey and found himself wide open.

Justin kicked a crisp lead pass to Ramon.

"Take it all the way, dude!" Justin shouted to Ramon.

Achmed, one of the Lightning's forwards, raced across the field and pulled up next to

Ramon. Achmed leaned in with a shoulder-to-shoulder charge, trying to force Ramon off the ball. But Ramon kept control and began to dribble away.

Suddenly Achmed launched his feet forward, going into a sliding tackle. His left foot slammed the ball away from Ramon, sending it right toward Joey. Joey trapped the speeding ball with his chest, then dribbled back toward Flyers' territory.

Crossing the center line, Joey spotted Achmed racing ahead on his right. He sent a waist-high driving pass to Achmed. Achmed trapped it with his thigh, then kept running, alternating feet on the dribble.

The Flyers' striker caught up to Achmed and pressed him with a shoulder-to-shoulder charge. But before the striker could push him off the ball, Achmed caught sight of his teammate Vicki. She was open and standing by the Flyers' penalty spot.

Achmed fired a pinpoint pass to Vicki. She kicked the ball right at the goal. Amanda dove toward the shot, but the ball sailed just inches over her outstretched arms. It slammed into the net at the back of the goal.

"Tie game!" Joey shouted, returning the high five Vicki had given him earlier.

"Told you guys!" Achmed said, smiling. "We are a killer team."

"Yeah, well, the game's not over yet, Killer," Ramon yelled, pointing at the clock. "There's still a minute and a half left to go."

"Let's do it, dude," Achmed shouted back at Ramon. Then he turned to his teammates. "One more goal, guys, and we will have mounted the most awesome comeback in soccer history."

Ramon shook his head. "'Most awesome comeback in soccer history,'" he repeated. "That is so lame."

As Vicki ran the ball out to the center

circle, the clock hit the one-minute mark.

Tyrone, the Flyers' striker, kicked the ball to Ramon to start play again. Ramon kicked it right back. Ricky Johnson, one of the Lightning's fullbacks, guarded Tyrone.

Dribbling into the Lightning's territory, Tyrone spotted his teammate, Jason, one of the Flyers' forwards. Jason was open. Tyrone caught the ball with the inside of his foot and sent a driving pass sailing toward Jason.

But Pablo Sanchez, the Lightning's midfielder, stole the pass and sped toward the Flyers' goal.

Three Flyers' defenders closed in on Pablo, who glanced left, then right, hoping to find an open teammate.

"Over here!" shouted Dmitri Petrovich, another Lightning midfielder, waving his arms frantically.

But Pablo was trapped. Three Flyers, Ramon, Andy, and Steve Mills, surrounded him. Pablo tried to maintain control of the ball, but it was a lost cause. Ramon finally kicked the ball away from Pablo.

Andy, the Flyers' sweeper, broke free from the pack and caught up to the ball. He dribbled back toward the Lightning's goal where Ernie Steele was waiting anxiously.

Andy shifted the ball from his left foot to his right and bypassed Vicki. Changing directions suddenly, he cut back to his left. He ran past Dmitri and then Pablo, who had hurried back on defense after losing the ball. Samantha "Sam" Pearce, the Lightning's sweeper, was their last line of defense.

Sam was not going to wait for Andy to come to her. She raced from her position at the top of the Lightning's penalty area, putting herself directly in Andy's path. Sam lunged for the ball with her left foot, but Andy reacted quickly. He came to a sudden stop, trapping the ball with his right foot. Sam stumbled past him, and Andy resumed his dribbling, charging forward.

Ernie was now all that stood between Andy and the tie-breaking goal.

Crossing into the penalty area, Andy angled to his left. Ernie, his eyes fixed on Andy's every movement, took a step in that direction. Andy cut to his right and Ernie slid back smoothly, following him.

Andy threw a head fake to the left, hoping that Ernie would fall for it and move that way, leaving the right side of the goal open. But Ernie stood his ground. It would take more than a simple fake to pull him out of position.

Andy continued pushing to his right, and Ernie adjusted with each step his opponent took. Then Andy suddenly cut to the left, stopped, and fired a left-footed shot toward the far-right corner of the goal.

Ernie, who had taken one quick step to his right, also stopped short when he saw Andy winding up for the kick. But the ball was in the air before he could step back to his left. He had only one chance to block the shot and keep the game tied.

Crouching slightly, then springing up and across the front of the goal, Ernie used every inch of his long gangly arms. Ernie's hand hit the ball just as it was about to cross the end line and enter the goal. He flicked his wrist and swatted the ball away.

"Yeah!" shouted Joey. "Nice save!"

"This is one time I'm glad my arms

are too long for my body," Ernie said, scrambling back to his feet. "Usually I feel like I swapped arms with a seven-foot-tall NBA center!"

Dmitri, the Lightning's midfielder, got to the ball just before Andy and kicked it downfield into Flyers' territory.

Pablo caught up to the ball at the same time as the Flyers' midfielder. They battled for possession. The midfielder finally managed to kick the ball to his teammate, Justin, who started charging back toward the Lightning's side of the field.

But Ricky, the Lightning's fullback, was ready for that and rushed over to help. With a shoulder-to-shoulder charge,

Ricky put enough space between Justin and the ball to get his own foot in and kick it back toward the Flyers' goal.

The ball zoomed back and forth across the field, first toward one goal and then toward the other, as the clock ticked down—forty seconds left, then thirty, and twenty. Losing was bad, but in some ways a tie was worse. It was like all the hard work everyone had just put in for forty minutes was for nothing. No one hated a tie more than Joey. At least in baseball there were extra innings, but unless it was a championship game, a soccer match that ended in a tie was just a tie.

Joey had the ball. He was just to the right of the center circle in Flyers' territory when the clock hit the ten-second mark. Joey charged forward. Ramon met him and tried a shoulder charge, but Joey reversed his direction and spun past him.

The clock ticked down to seven seconds.

Joey spotted Dmitri across the field. He sprinted to the left side of the penalty area. With a mighty kick, Joey launched a line drive pass that sailed across the field. Dmitri trapped the ball with his chest. It bounced once, then he launched a rising shot to the right side of the goal.

Amanda leaped up and across, but the ball was moving too fast. It zipped past her fingertips and bounced into the goal.

Three seconds—two—one. Game over. Final score: Lightning 4, Flyers 3.

The Lightning all ran over to

Dmitri, cheering wildly, as Amanda walked dejectedly toward the sideline.

Dmitri broke away from his teammates' group hug and offered a high five to the Flyers' goalie. "Nice game, Amanda," he said. "You worked really hard out there."

Amanda nodded and slapped Dmitri's hand. "Thanks," she said. "Sometimes being a goalie just stinks."

"Nah," said Ernie, who had trotted over from the other end of the field. "Month-old cheese stinks. Being a goalie is fun."

Amanda laughed. No one could resist Ernie's goofy jokes and puns. "Besides," Ernie continued, "you'll get a chance for a rematch in the big tournament."

"And there's no way you'll beat us there," Ramon chimed in, walking over.

Both teams were excited about the upcoming soccer tournament. Teams from all of the nearby towns participated every year. The whole tournament was organized by the players themselves, and both the Flyers and the Lightning were really looking forward to it.

"I can't wait for this tournament," said Joey, who bumped fists with Ramon. "It's gonna be awesome."

"That's too bad, then," said a voice from behind the group.

Joey spun around and saw his friend and teammate Tony Delvecchio strolling up to the players. Tony was a member of the Lightning, but he hadn't been able to play that afternoon.

"What do you mean, 'too bad'?" Achmed asked. "Joey's right. The tournament's gonna be amazing."

"There isn't going to be a tournament," Tony said flatly. "The tournament's been canceled!"

Chapter Two

"Canceled?" Achmed cried. "Who canceled it?"

"A water pipe that runs under Miller's Field, that's who," Tony replied.

"What *are* you talking about?!" Ernie asked.

"I just walked past Miller's Field and there are repair dudes with big machines digging the whole field up," Tony explained. "There was water everywhere, so I asked what was going on and they told me that an underground water pipe burst. Looks like the field is going to be off-limits for a long time."

"But we always have the tournament at

Miller's Field," Steve complained. "It's like a tradition."

"It's the nicest field, too," Joey added. "Way nicer than our field."

"Yeah," Ramon agreed. "And the tournament is only a couple of weeks away!"

"Did you guys hear a word Tony said?" Vicki asked, rolling her eyes. "There isn't going to be a tournament. Miller's Field is ruined."

"Why can't we have the tournament right here on our field?" Pablo suggested.

"No way," Joey replied. "It's just not good enough. I mean, Miller's Field is beautiful and it has chalk lines and nice bleachers. This is just a plain old field. And it's too small. If we tell kids that the tournament is going to be here, nobody will show up."

"Joey's right!" Vicki shouted. "No one is going to want to play a big tournament on our crummy field."

"There just isn't going to be a tournament this year," Ricky added sadly. "And there's nothing we can do about it."

Players from both teams hung around for a little while longer, grumbling about the loss of their tournament. Joey was especially disappointed. Even though the tournament was just an informal series of games, it always made him feel like a pro.

"See you guys," he said, waving good-bye halfheartedly before turning and heading for home.

That evening at home, Dmitri sat in front of his computer typing furiously. *Joey and the others are wrong*, he thought to himself. *Our field's not that bad. There's plenty of room for five teams. And I think that kids'll show up.*

Dmitri was a computer whiz, and he loved to organize clubs and teams. For him, organizing the tournament came naturally. He quickly designed a simple website for the tournament, so the teams and the rest of the community would know what had happened.

He sent out e-mails to all the teams who usually showed up to let everyone know about the disaster at Miller's Field. And he asked all the teams if they would want to hold the tournament at the Lightning's home field instead.

This is definitely a win-win situation, he thought as he put the finishing touches on the website. *If no one wants to play on our field, we're no worse off than we are now. But if the teams agree to play there, then I just saved the tournament.*

The next day, the Lightning decided to hold their usual practice session. Everyone was disappointed about the tournament being canceled, but they all still loved playing soccer. Even though it looked as if they were only going to play another regular game against the Flyers, they wanted to be ready.

At the time Dmitri left his house to go to the practice, he hadn't yet heard back from any of the teams. He decided not to tell his friends that he had put up the website, just in case he was wrong and the teams really didn't want to hold the tournament on the Lightning's field. No one had to know if he was wrong, but if he were right, he'd be a hero for saving the tournament.

"Ready? Go!" Achmed shouted as he raced along the middle of the field, dribbling the ball. Vicki was running just ahead of him, about ten yards away. They were working on a team passing drill. Two players at a time took turns running the length of the field while passing the ball back and forth to each other. "It's all yours, Vicki!"

Achmed fired a pass just slightly ahead of Vicki. She caught up with the ball and gained control. Then Achmed sped up, running a few yards ahead of Vicki. She returned the ball to him with a crisp pass of her own.

"Nice one, Vicki," Achmed called out as he caught up to Vicki's pass.

"Yeah," Vicki shouted back. "Too bad we don't have a tournament to use it in."

"I know," Ernie said sadly. "This is going to be the first time in three years that we don't have one."

"I can't believe it. I was really looking forward to getting back at Fairfield for beating us in the final game last year, too," Vicki added. "We would have kicked butt against them this time. We're all playing better. Even Ernie's making some great saves out there, like the one he made yesterday against the Flyers."

"Thank you, thank you," Ernie said, bowing deeply. "Your confidence in me is overwhelming."

"You know what I mean," said Vicki,

playfully punching him in the arm.

"Hey, watch it with that stuff," Ernie said. "That's the arm I use to make all those great saves . . . which I won't be making in the tournament."

"Just playing another regular old game against Ramon and those guys won't be the same," Vicki pointed out.

Dmitri and Joey were up next. Dmitri didn't want to tell his friends about the website. He didn't want to get anyone's hopes up and he certainly didn't want anyone to know if no one actually replied. Dmitri launched a low pass to Joey, who trapped it, dribbled a few steps, then fired it right back.

A team dribbling drill was up next. The players formed two lines about twenty yards away from one another. Tony Delvecchio started things off. Although Tony had missed the last game, he was one of the team's best players.

"I'm glad we were smart enough not to have the tournament on our field," Tony said as he alternated the dribble from his left foot to his right. "Could you picture fitting all those people here?" He reached the other line of players and dropped the ball off for Sam.

"What people? It's just five teams," Sam said as she picked up the dribble with her right foot and headed back in the direction Tony had just come from.

"It wouldn't be just the players, Sam," Tony replied.

"Tony's right," Ricky said, taking the ball from Sam and dribbling back across the field. "Along with all the kids who play, you got families, friends, fans. You know the drill." Ricky finished his dribbling and let the ball roll to Joey.

"Yeah," Joey chimed in, trapping the ball, then dribbling it back. "Everybody's mom, dad, and third cousin once removed would show up."

"I had to remove my third cousin once," Ernie joked. "He was making too much noise at Thanksgiving dinner."

Dmitri didn't laugh. He was starting to get nervous. He hadn't thought about all the people who would show up for the tournament. He thought he had done a good thing setting up the website and contacting everyone. Now he wasn't so sure. What if the teams all agreed? What would he do then? He tried to calm down—the website had only been up for one night. No one had probably even seen it yet!

Shooting practice was next—for everyone but Ernie. For him, shooting practice meant goalkeeping practice.

"Okay, gang, let's see what you got," Ernie announced as he set himself just in front of the goal.

Joey stood off to the side holding a ball. Two additional balls sat on the ground next to him. "Ready?" he shouted. "Go!"

Joey rolled the first ball toward the goal. Pablo, at the head of the line, dashed toward the moving ball. Ernie shuffled to the side, hoping to cut off the angle on Pablo's shot. Pablo reached the ball, planted his left foot, and kicked a hard shot toward the goal.

The ball sped in a low line drive, rising as it moved to just above Ernie's knees. Not wanting to allow the ball to get through his legs, Ernie dropped to both knees and caught the ball chest high. "Nothing gets by the Big E!" Ernie boasted. Then he rolled the ball back out to Joey.

As Ernie made the save, Joey rolled the second ball toward the goal. Vicki, next in line, hurried toward it. She sent a bouncing shot skipping toward the left side of the goal.

Ernie jumped back to his feet in time to slide to his right and knock the shot away with the bottom of his shoe. Then he bounded back up to be ready for the next shot.

Dmitri's turn came next, but his mind really wasn't on shooting practice. He was more worried about getting home to take down the website. He kicked the ball so hard it sailed over Ernie's head, over the back of the goal, and rolled completely off the field.

"How many goals are you trying to score with one shot, Dmitri?" Ernie asked as Joey ran to get the ball. "It's just one goal per shot, no matter how hard you kick it."

"Hmm, what?" Dmitri asked, not even realizing that he had just blasted the ball over the net. "Sorry, maybe someone else should go. I, um, I actually have to get home. I'll see you guys." Then Dmitri ran off the field.

"What's up with him?" Vicki asked.

"Don't know," Joey said, scratching his head. "Maybe we should all just call it a day."

"That's what I call it," Ernie quipped. "Until the sun goes down. Then I call it a night."

The Lightning said their good-byes and headed off the field.

Dmitri ran practically all the way home. Breathing hard and sweating even more than he had on the soccer field, he raced up the stairs to his room.

He turned his computer on. *This is so not good*, he thought as he waited for his computer to boot up. It felt as if it were taking three times longer than usual. *If the teams don't want to play on our field, then there really won't be a tournament. But if they do, how will we fit everyone?*

His computer finally booted up and he went to the website he had created. Dmitri stared at the monitor in disbelief. His heart began to pound. Not only had the five original teams agreed to play in the tournament, but also a total of sixteen teams from all over the area had signed up. His plan had worked too well.

It didn't take a genius to figure out that the Lightning's field—good old small Field Number Four in the municipal park—was not going to be big enough to host what had quickly become a monster tournament.

"What have I gotten us into?" Dmitri muttered in horror.

Chapter Three

"You did what?!" Vicki shouted at Dmitri the next afternoon when he had finished explaining to his friends what he had done. The team had gathered at Field Number Four for another practice.

"I thought I was helping," Dmitri replied sheepishly. "I figured that we had nothing to lose by asking. I hadn't thought about all the people who come along with the team. And I never thought that so many teams would want to play."

"How could you just do that without telling us?" Tony shouted.

"I didn't think it could hurt," Dmitri said.

"Yeah, well, you were wrong!" Tony shot back. "Now we're committed and people are counting on us. What are we supposed to do?"

"Take it easy, guys," Joey said, trying to calm everyone down. "Let's just figure this out."

"What's there to figure out?" Tony asked. "We can't just back out. Everyone is gonna be so psyched that we saved the tournament. We can't let them all down."

"If we don't figure out something, we'll never be able to show our faces on a soccer field again," Sam said.

"We could wear football helmets so no one would recognize us," Ernie suggested, hoping to lighten the mood a little, but no one laughed.

"Let's try to stay calm," said Vicki. "We're just going to have to find another field."

"There are no other fields!" Ricky shouted.

"What about the school field?" Pablo suggested hopefully. "That's big enough."

"No good, Pabs," Joey replied. "The school team always plays on the weekend."

"How about Rogers Stadium?" Sam suggested. "That's not far from here, and it sure is big enough."

"Rogers Stadium?" Tony repeated. "The stadium where the Stingers play? Are you nuts? They're a semipro team. They'd never just let a bunch of kids play there. We'd have to pay, like, a million bucks to rent the place."

"Let's see," Ernie said, digging into his pocket. He pulled out a crumpled dollar bill and a fistful of change. "I've got a dollar sixty-three. Does that help?"

Dmitri, who had been pacing back and forth along the sidelines, stepped into the middle of the group. "Wait a second!" he yelled to get everyone's attention. "I have an idea. Remember that really old field on the far side of this park?"

"You mean Field Number Ten?" Joey asked.

"Yup," Dmitri replied. "Where the Stingers played before they built Rogers Stadium. If it was big enough for a semipro team, it's got to be big enough for us. And it's probably big enough to divide into two fields, so that two games can be going on at the same time."

"But no one's used that field for years, dude," Tony pointed out.

"Exactly," Dmitri said. "So it's got to be available."

"It's also probably a mess," Vicki added. "No one ever uses it, so the Parks Department doesn't keep it up."

"It's gonna be horrible," Ricky complained. "And then we won't have a tournament, and the other kids will hate us, and—"

"Come on, guys," Dmitri pleaded with his friends. "Can we just take a look? How bad can it be?"

"We might as well," Joey agreed. "It's only across the park. And it's not like we've got a bunch of other places to choose from."

The Lightning hurried across their own field, then cut through a wooded area of the park. After passing several baseball diamonds, tennis courts, and basketball hoops, they came to an enormous soccer field, at least three times the size of Field Number Four. A locked chain-link fence surrounded the field.

Dmitri's spirits sank at the sight of the field. It was overgrown with weeds and wildflowers. Several tree branches had fallen onto the field from the bordering woods. There was litter and garbage everywhere, and the goals were long gone. A long line of bleachers, in serious need of a paint job, ran along the side of the messy field.

"Well, it could be worse," Ernie said, breaking the uncomfortable silence.

"Really?" Vicki asked. "How?"

"Um . . . it could be flooded, too," Ernie replied.

"Well, obviously the first thing we have to do is get in there," Dmitri said, peering through the fence. He yanked on a huge padlock, which dangled from a gate in the fence. The lock didn't budge. "We need to get the key."

"And how are we gonna do that?" Tony asked, kicking away an old soda can.

"There's a ranger station at the northern end of the park," Dmitri explained. "They'll probably have the key there. Come on."

"You think they'll just give the key to a bunch of kids?" Vicki asked skeptically.

"Only one way to find out," Dmitri said. He turned and started walking away from the field. No one followed. He stopped and turned back to his friends. "Am I going to have to clean up this whole field by myself?"

"No," Joey said. "I'm with you. Come on."

One by one, Dmitri's friends shuffled off toward the ranger station.

"I think this could be okay," Dmitri said, trying to convince himself as much as his friends. "We have five whole days before the tournament. That's plenty of time to clean the field up and make it look great."

"Yeah, maybe it'll look so good when

we get through with it that the Stingers will want to move back here and *we* can use Rogers Stadium!" Ernie said enthusiastically.

"Right, Ernie," said Vicki, rolling her eyes. "And maybe you'll get signed by the Los Angeles Galaxy so you can play next to Beckham."

"Hey! It could happen!" Ernie shot back defensively.

The group soon approached a small brick building. Through the building's one tiny window, Dmitri spotted a park ranger sitting at a desk.

"Okay, he's there," Dmitri said hopefully. *Maybe this is going to work out after all,* he thought.

"I'll do the talking," Joey said, stepping up to the front of the group.

"No," Dmitri insisted. "I got us into this, and using Field Ten was my idea. I'll talk to the ranger. I'll get us into that field."

Joey nodded. Dmitri opened the door to the ranger station and stepped in, followed by the rest of his Lightning teammates. The group took up every inch of space in the tiny office.

"Can I help you kids?" the ranger asked, looking suspiciously at the group.

"Yes, sir," Dmitri said nervously. "You see, we're the Lightning. I mean, that's our soccer team."

"Yeah, we're 5 and 0 this year so far," Tony added proudly.

"Just let Dmitri talk, Tony, will ya," Vicki said, poking Tony in the shoulder.

"Anyway, we have to host this soccer tournament," Dmitri continued. "But the field we usually play on, Field Four, is way too small."

"Get to the point already, Dmitri," Tony said. "Ask him about the key!"

"Right," Dmitri said. "The key. See, the thing is we would like to clean up Field Number Ten so that we—"

"Field Ten?" the ranger interrupted. "That's been fenced off for years. Nobody uses that."

"We know," Dmitri said patiently. "But we'd like to clean it up ourselves and use it for our tournament. We'll do all the work. Really. All the teams are counting on us and we don't really have anywhere else we can play. So, what I'm asking is, may we please have the key to the lock so we can get in there and clean it up?" Dmitri flashed a big smile, trying to hide how nervous he felt.

"Just like that," the ranger said, shaking his head. "I give you the key and you go in and clean up the field?"

"Yes, sir. That's our plan," Dmitri replied.

"I'm sorry, son, but it just doesn't work that way," the ranger said. "You can't clean up the field without a permit."

"You need a permit to clean something up?" Vicki asked.

"You need a permit to make any changes to city property—even if they are good changes," the ranger explained. "The city council issues them."

"The city council!" Tony shouted. "They'll never give a permit to a bunch of kids. Forget it. This is not going to work. There isn't going to be a tournament. And we're the ones who are gonna have to let everybody down," added Tony, glaring at Dmitri.

Dmitri turned and started for the door.

"Now wait a minute, son," the ranger said.

Dmitri turned back and looked at the ranger hopefully.

"It's true that giving a permit to a bunch of kids is a bit unusual," the ranger began, rubbing his chin. "But you might have a chance if you can show the council that you've got the community behind you."

"What do you mean?" Vicki asked.

"Well, get some donations, contributions," the ranger explained. "Show the council that you've got local shop owners on your side. You'll need paint and brushes, litter bags and lawn mowers, stuff like that. That'll show the council that you're serious, that you've put some effort into this thing already. Then, if they say yes, you'll have the supplies you need. I'm not giving you any guarantees, mind you, but if you're serious about this . . ."

"Yes, sir, we're serious," Dmitri said quickly. "We love soccer, and we really want this tournament to happen. Do you know when the next city council meeting is?"

"Well, let's see," the ranger said, pulling his calendar off the wall. "Here it is. The next meeting is three days from now."

"Three days!" Tony shouted. "But even if they say yes, that only leaves us one day to clean up the field! Do you understand what that means?"

"I understand," Vicki said dejectedly. "I understand that there's not going to be a tournament!"

Chapter Four

"That's it then," Tony said, throwing up his hands as they left the ranger station.

"No!" Dmitri said firmly. "We can do this."

"Come on, Dmitri, give it up!" Tony yelled. "You messed up and that's that."

"Hey, it's not Dmitri's fault the water pipe under Miller's Field broke," Joey said. "Cut him some slack, Tony. Dmitri was just trying to help."

"Okay," Tony admitted, looking at Dmitri. "You were just trying to help. I get it. But where does that leave us now?"

"That leaves us with two days to get ready," Dmitri said. "So here's the plan.

We've got to go to all the stores in town for donations. We need paint and painting supplies, lawn mowers, garbage bags, and work gloves. Anything you can think of. And don't forget, ask the store owners to sign a list of the stuff they agree to give us so we can show it to the city council."

"I know Ralph at the hardware store," Joey said. "My dad shops there all the time. I'll see what he's willing to donate."

"We bring the mower into Mr. Walton at the garden store for repairs," Ernie explained. "I can see if he'll donate one of those big rider mowers."

"Okay guys, we've got two days," Dmitri said. He was still worried, but he was also beginning to feel a little hopeful that this plan might actually work. "Let's do it!"

The Lightning spent the next two days trying to round up donations. Dmitri knew that it was a long shot—even if they got local store owners to donate enough supplies, there was no guarantee that the city council would give them a permit.

Tony was right about one thing, Dmitri thought as he walked up to the local sporting goods store. *We are just "a bunch of kids."* He took a deep breath, then stepped into the store, hoping he could convince the owner to donate some brand-new soccer goals.

Late in the afternoon the day before the town meeting, the Lightning all met up at Field Number Four. When the rest of the kids arrived, they found Dmitri and Tony kicking around a soccer ball. But the two friends didn't seem too enthusiastic.

"Okay!" Joey announced, waving a piece of paper in the air. "Ralph's Hardware has signed on to give us paint and brushes. It didn't take much to convince Ralph that he'd be helping out the community. He liked that, I guess, because he gave me the stuff."

"I got us a couple of lawn mowers from the garden supply store," Ernie said, smiling and holding up his signed agreement. "Mr. Walton liked the idea of making a place for all the kids to play."

"Nice work, guys," Dmitri said. "It didn't take long to convince Mr. Gold at the sporting goods store to give us the goals. Turns out he's a big soccer fan. He's got season tickets for all the Stingers' home games."

"Then why don't you guys look happy?" Vicki asked.

"Because it all means nothing if they don't give us that permit tomorrow," Tony explained. "Just because a few store owners were nice to us doesn't mean the city council is gonna listen to a bunch of kids."

"Tony's right," Dmitri said anxiously. "Even if the council does give us a permit, we'll only have one day to fix up that field. It might not be possible. But what else can we do?"

"We can play a little soccer," Ernie said, stealing the ball from Tony and firing a pass right to Achmed. "Remember soccer?"

"Let's see that ball, Achmed!" Vicki shouted, joining in on the game.

Achmed launched a pass to Vicki. She trapped it with her leg and began dribbling.

One by one, all the kids joined in. Sam tried to steal the ball from Vicki, who kicked it to Pablo. There were no set drills, but that was okay. The Lightning were on the soccer field, kicking the ball, and, for the moment, that was all that mattered.

"Go for the save, Ernie!" Achmed shouted, firing the ball right at Ernie.

Ernie, standing in the middle of the field, dove for the ball and swatted it away. "That's got to be the first save in soccer history ever to be made without a goal!"

The ball zipped from player to player. For the moment, at least, the Lightning had

forgotten about the big meeting the next day
and had gotten caught up in their love for
the game.

As the playing slowed down and it began
to get dark, the mood once again turned sour.
"That *was* fun," Tony admitted. "Let's just
hope we get to do it again in a few days. On
Field Number Ten."

"Yeah," Dmitri sighed, starting to feel
very nervous about the next day. "On Field
Number Ten."

Chapter Five

The town hall was packed the following day as Dmitri and his friends filed in and found seats.

One thought kept going through Dmitri's mind. *Just a bunch of kids. They're going to say, "You're just a bunch of kids."*

The meeting was called to order and Dmitri felt his stomach tighten with nerves. After a few people brought up problems, and a number of votes were taken, Mr. Rose, the head of the city council, spoke up.

"Is there any other business for the city council today?" he said in a loud, clear voice.

Dmitri stood up and stepped forward.

"Yes, sir," he said. "I have a request."

Mr. Rose looked over the top of his half-rimmed glasses at the boy standing before him. "And who are you, young man?"

"My name is Dmitri Petrovich and I'm here with my soccer team."

"And what business do you have with the city council, young man?" Mr. Rose asked.

"Well, sir, we have a soccer tournament every year," Dmitri continued, his heart pounding as he spoke. "Usually we play at Miller's Field. But this year there is a broken water pipe there."

"I'm aware of that, young man," Mr. Rose said impatiently.

"Yes, sir. We need a field big enough to host the tournament. And the only one in town that's big enough is Field Number Ten in the municipal park. But the field is a mess. So I—I mean we—my teammates and I—would like a permit to clean up the field."

Dmitri took a deep breath. He had managed to say what he wanted to say. Now all he could do was wait for the answer.

Mr. Rose took off his glasses and stared down at Dmitri. "Am I to understand that you want this council to give a permit to a bunch of kids to clean up a soccer field?"

Dmitri's heart sank.

"And how do you kids intend to do this?" Mr. Rose continued without waiting for an answer. "What supplies and equipment do you have? What will you use to collect garbage, cut grass, and everything else that is needed? Do you have any idea what's involved in such a cleanup? Have you thought this through, young man?"

"Yes, sir, we have," Dmitri said, holding out the papers that the shopkeepers had signed. "My friends and I have gone to local shop owners. They've pledged to donate equipment to help us with the cleanup."

"Bring them over here," Mr. Rose said.

Dmitri handed the papers to Mr. Rose.

"Well, this is all well and good, but it seems a waste to fix up a field for one tournament. No one has needed or used that field for years, and I doubt anyone will need it again," Mr. Rose finally said.

Dmitri thought for a moment, then said, "We might just be a bunch of kids, sir, but we can make a real difference to the park and the whole community. This is not just about us. We can turn that junky field into a great place for kids. I think once the field is fixed up, lots of kids will want to use it. I know plenty of kids—and adults—who love soccer as much as we do, and I know they would appreciate a nice big field to play on. The whole community is behind us. That's why they all agreed to pitch in—because this is for them, too. For everyone in town. So if you give us the permit, we'll turn that old field into something that the whole town can be proud of! Thank you!"

All of Dmitri's teammates jumped to their feet and started to applaud loudly.

"Way to go, dude!" Tony yelled out.

"Good stuff!" Ernie shouted. "You should run for class president, Dmitri!"

"Quiet!" Mr. Rose shouted. "If you don't settle down, I'll have to ask you all to leave!"

The kids stopped applauding and quickly took their seats.

"There will be a brief recess while the council considers this request for a permit," Mr. Rose said sharply.

Everyone hurried out into the hallway.

"You were awesome!" Vicki said to Dmitri, patting him on the back. "You sounded like a lawyer on a TV show."

"Yeah, well, we'll see how awesome I was in a few minutes," Dmitri said, worried that all the effort he and his friends had put in might still be for nothing. He wished that he had never put up the tournament website. "I don't think Mr. Rose likes me."

"He doesn't have to be your friend, Dmitri," Joey said. "He just has to give us the permit."

"Yeah, it would be all kinds of bad if he says no," Achmed said.

"We'd have to tell everyone that there's not going to be a tournament," Sam added.

"We know that, guys!" Dmitri snapped. "We just have to wait."

"This waiting is killing me," Tony said, pacing from one side of the hall to the other.

Dmitri started to sweat. He kept replaying the scene in his head, wondering if there was something more he could have done or said. Ten minutes later, the door flew open and the kids were let back into the council chamber.

Mr. Rose walked in through a door in

the back of the room and sat down. "Mr. Petrovich, please step forward," he said.

Dmitri stood and walked toward Mr. Rose, whose face showed no sign of what he had decided.

"Young man, the city council has carefully considered your request," he began.

Oh, no, he's going to turn me down, Dmitri thought. *He's going to say no!*

"And in light of the effort you have already put into the project, and your ability to involve members of the community, the city council has decided to grant your request. Here is your permit, young man. Good luck."

The entire council chamber erupted into cheers. Dmitri's friends mobbed him, jumping up and down as if he had just scored a game-winning goal.

"You did it, dude!" Tony shouted as the group charged out of the council chamber.

Dmitri could hardly believe it. He felt like a giant weight had been lifted from his shoulders—at least he did until he remembered what a mess the field still was.

"Guys, listen up!" Dmitri shouted once they were all outside. "This is great. But don't forget, we still have to fix up the whole field. And we only have one day to do it!"

"Wow," Joey said glumly. "I've been so busy worrying about just getting the permit, I didn't even think about that."

"Well, it's time to start thinking about that," Dmitri said anxiously. "I'll see you all tomorrow . . . early, at Field Number Ten. I just hope we can get this done!"

Chapter Six

Early the next morning, the Lightning met at Field Number Ten. They had their permit, equipment and supplies, and the key to the field. The big cleanup was about to begin.

First the garbage had to be picked up. Everyone spread out and began picking up trash, but by the time they were done, half the morning had slipped away.

Mowing and scraping came next. After a

few more hours, the gang took a break.

"I'm tired," said Ernie, turning off the mower and flopping down onto the ground. "No wonder I don't like doing this at home."

"My hand is killing me from scraping the paint off these bleachers," Vicki complained. She looked down the long row of benches and shook her head. "That's all we've done? Jeez! We've been here for hours and there's, like, a million miles of bleachers left to scrape."

"Yeah," added Ricky, who put down his scraper, too. "And then we have to paint the whole thing."

"Man, that is one big field!" Ernie said. "We've only cleared a little piece of it!"

"Who are we kidding?!" Tony cried. "We'll never get this done in time! The tournament is supposed to start tomorrow morning."

"Do you just want to quit?" Dmitri asked Tony softly. He had no more strength to argue. And maybe Tony was right. Maybe this was all one big waste of time.

"We just have so much left to do," Vicki admitted, flopping down onto the ground, tossing her scraper aside.

"Maybe a few extra hands will help," said a voice from behind the bleachers.

"Ramon!" Dmitri cried. "What are you doing here?"

"Hey, you guys aren't the only ones who care about this tournament," Ramon explained as he and the rest of the Flyers strolled out onto the field. "The Flyers want it just as badly as the Lightning. We heard what you were doing and we want to help you get the field ready, so we can beat you in the tournament tomorrow."

"Hey, Ramon," Vicki shouted, hopping back up to her feet and waving her scraper back and forth. "Ever use one of these?"

"Nope," Ramon replied.

"Well, there's a first time for everything," she said, pulling a second scraper out of her pocket and tossing it to Ramon. "You start at the other end of the bleachers. I'll meet you in the middle."

VROOOOM! VROOOOM!

The deafening sound of a roaring engine drowned out every other noise.

"I brought my dad's rider mower!" Steve Mills shouted to be heard over the engine noise. He rode onto the field, followed by Andy Turner and Amanda Wilson. "Where do I start?"

Dmitri smiled and pointed to a section of the field that Ernie hadn't mowed yet. "Welcome to the team!" he shouted.

"What?" Steve yelled back.

Dmitri laughed and pointed again.

The arrival of the Flyers got everyone charged up. Field Number Ten was a flurry of activity. And Dmitri started to feel as if they just might be ready in time.

A short while later, several cars and trucks pulled up to the field. Out stepped Ralph from the hardware store, Mr. Walton from the garden store, and Mr. Gold from the sporting goods store.

"We thought you kids could use a little extra help," Mr. Gold said, picking up a paintbrush. "It's looking pretty good already."

"Seems like everyone's pitching in," Mr. Walton said, looking across the field.

The park ranger who had given the kids the key was heading in their direction.

"This field has been a mess for so long, I'm glad to see it fixed up," the ranger said. "Let me give you a hand."

With all of the extra hands, the pace of the

work picked up and the field began to take shape.

A little while later, an official city car pulled up. Out stepped Mr. Rose, the head of the city council. Dmitri panicked.

"Oh, no!" Dmitri cried. "They changed their minds! He's here to tell me that this was all one big mistake, that he's taking back the permit and we can't use the field after all!"

"Mr. Petrovich," Mr. Rose said, walking over to Dmitri.

"Yes, sir?" Dmitri said, shaking nervously.

"After what you said at the meeting yesterday . . ."

"Yes?"

"I was wondering if you could use an extra pair of hands," Mr. Rose said, rolling up his sleeves.

"Sure!" Dmitri said, feeling relieved. "Thanks!"

A few hours later, the field was just about ready.

"I brought along the finishing touch," Mr. Gold announced, pulling a line marker out of the back of his truck.

"Awesome!" yelled Achmed.

The line marker was a box filled with chalk dust, on wheels with a lawn-mower-type handle. As the marker rolled along, chalk came out, creating a line. "We are going to look like pros out there!"

When the last section of the field had finally been mowed, the players all lined up and took turns pushing the line marker. The full outline of two fields, side by side, was marked off first. Then the goal areas, penalty areas, center circle, and center line were chalked up on each field. Finally, Mr. Gold helped Dmitri put the goals he had contributed in place.

"That's it!" Dmitri announced. "We made it. We're all set for the tournament tomorrow." Then he turned to everyone who had just worked so hard. "Thank you all for showing up."

"You kids deserve it," Mr. Rose said, smiling. "And we'll see you tomorrow at the tournament."

"You're coming?" Dmitri asked, very surprised.

"Wouldn't miss it!" Mr. Rose replied.

"Yeah, well I've had enough of this one-big-happy-family stuff!" Ramon said to Dmitri. "Tomorrow, we're the Lightning and the Flyers again, so get ready for the real competition."

Chapter Seven

The big day had finally arrived. Dmitri
and his teammates met up at Field Number
Ten hours before the first game of the
tournament was scheduled to start. The
freshly painted bleachers gleamed in the
bright sunshine. Colorful streamers waved
from the top of the fence, which was now
wide-open to let in the crowd. And the two
fields, with their close-cropped grass, crisp
white chalk lines, and brand-new goals,
looked good enough to host a pro game.

Soon, players from the other teams
began to arrive, along with their friends
and families. Dmitri, Ramon, and all their

teammates beamed with pride as everyone oohed and aahed at the beautiful field they had worked so hard to prepare.

"You kids did all this yourselves?" Ernie's dad asked when he arrived and took his seat in the bleachers, which were quickly filling up. "I remember what this field used to look like. Man, this is really something."

"Yup," Ernie replied. "It's amazing what a little hard work can do."

"Really?" Mr. Steele said. "Can I quote you on that when it's time to mow *our* lawn?"

"Uh, I gotta go, Dad," Ernie said quickly. "I got a game."

Mr. Rose was among the first to arrive. He found a seat in the bleachers. Within a few minutes he was joined by Mr. Walton, Mr. Gold, Ralph, and the park ranger.

As another game took place on the next field, the Lightning played their first game against a younger team who were in the tournament for the first time. The Lightning played crisply, passing and shooting and playing tight defense. Ernie made save after save, and the Lightning won the game 5–0.

For their second game, the Lightning played Fairfield, the team that had beaten them in the finals the year before. And, as Vicki had predicted, the Lightning beat Fairfield 4–2.

When the first day of play came to a close, the Lightning and the Flyers, who had also won their first two games, had both advanced to the semifinal round, which would take place the following day.

"Heading for another showdown," Ramon said to Joey as the teams packed up and headed home. "The Lightning and the Flyers. See ya in the final game."

"I wouldn't have it any other way!" Joey replied. "Just make sure you win your first game tomorrow so you can play us!"

"You can count on it," Ramon said.

The next morning, the teams met at the field. As the players warmed up, Vicki noticed a group of guys wearing Stingers jackets stepping up onto the bleachers.

"Hey!" she shouted to her teammates. "That's Billy Connors, the goalie for the Stingers! I've seen his picture in the paper." She raced over to the pro players. "Hey, Billy!"

"Hey, you guys did an amazing job fixing up our old field," Billy said as he took a seat next to his teammates. "We heard there was some great soccer going on in this tournament, so we came to watch the finals."

"Awesome!" Achmed cried.

The Lightning and the Flyers both won their semifinal games, setting up a showdown of the two rivals in the final game. Dmitri was so proud of his team. It made it that much better that after all of their hard work to save the tournament, they might win the whole thing.

Ramon battled Achmed for control of the ball at the kickoff. The championship game was underway.

Achmed pressed his shoulder against Ramon's and slipped his right foot between Ramon's foot and the ball. Gaining control of the ball, Achmed sped toward the Flyers' goal. Ramon chased him.

Achmed spotted Vicki near the right side of the Flyers' penalty area. He sent a driving kick soaring through the air toward her. Vicki trapped the ball with her shoulder and dribbled right at Amanda, who set herself in the goal.

Vicki went left and Amanda followed. Hoping to use Amanda's momentum against her, Vicki stopped short, then fired a shot toward the right side of the goal.

Amanda changed direction as quickly as she could. She dove back to the right side of the goal, but the ball zipped past her and struck the net at the back of the goal.

"Score!" shouted Joey, who raced over to Vicki and gave her a high five. "Nice shot."

Tyrone kicked the ball back into play for the Flyers, who charged down the field toward the Lightning's goal. Steve controlled the dribble and sent a sharp pass across the field to Justin, who took two steps, then launched the ball back to Steve. The ball ping-ponged back and forth between the two Flyers as they came closer and closer to the Lightning's goal.

Ernie crouched in the center of the Lightning's goal, trying to both relax and focus at the same time. As the ball whizzed back and forth between Steve and Justin, Ernie slid to his left, then back to the right.

Steve entered the Lightning's penalty area from the left side, sending Ernie scurrying to his right. Then Steve stopped suddenly and stepped away from the ball.

Justin was right behind him. He sent a rising shot angling toward the upper-right corner of the goal.

Ernie sprang up from his crouch and batted the ball away before it got close to crossing into the goal. But Steve, who knew that all of Ernie's focus would be on Justin, had slipped over to the right side of the goal. He was waiting in case Ernie made the save. Steve trapped the ball with his leg, then instantly fired another shot at the goal.

Ernie slid across the front of the goal and blocked the low shot with his body. He had hoped to catch it to slow things down a bit, but the ball bounced off his knee and rolled back out into play.

Ramon was waiting. "Thanks, Ernie!" he shouted, kicking a screaming line drive right back to the goal. This time Ernie dropped to one knee and caught the ball. He smothered it with his long arms, clutching it to his chest.

"This is as close to a break as I'm going to get," Ernie said. He stayed down on one knee for a moment to catch his breath.

Then he found Pablo open and tossed the ball out to him, sending the action back down toward the Flyers' side of the field.

Pablo dribbled across the center line into Flyers' territory, then kicked a driving pass to Vicki, who redirected the ball to Joey. Tony was sprinting toward the goal. Just as they had done in practice, Joey sent a lead pass a few steps in front of Tony. Tony caught up to the ball and launched a low shot at the goal.

Amanda had it played perfectly. She sank

to both knees and caught the ball. Her toss
to put the ball back in play was intended for
her teammate Andy, but Ricky cut in front
of Andy and stole the ball. Ricky dribbled
for two steps then fired a high shot just as
time ran out in the first half. The shot would
count if it got past Amanda.

It didn't.

Amanda was on her game. She stepped
to her right, jumped, and swatted the
ball away. The first half ended with the
Lightning clinging to a 1–0 lead.

During the halftime break, the players flopped down on the ground to rest. They drank lots of water and ate oranges and energy bars.

"You are a steel wall out there, Ernie," Joey said between gulps of water. "Get it? A 'Steele' wall."

"I get it," Ernie replied, laughing. "But Amanda's been just as tough. I'm glad you got that one goal past her, Vicki. That might be all we get."

"It's going to be all we need, too, Big E," Achmed said. "You are on fire out there!"

"Yeah, well, if you guys keep the ball down at the other end of the field, you'll make me look like a superstar," Ernie said.

As the second half got underway, the pattern of tight defense and back-and-forth play continued. The ball changed hands even more often than it had in the first half. Both teams had fewer shot opportunities. Ernie and Amanda stayed tough, rejecting the handful of shots that were actually taken.

As the clock ticked down to the game's final minute, and the score held at 1–0, Ernie thought of Achmed's words: *It's going to be all we need.*

Ernie was starting to think that Achmed may have been right.

There was nothing more satisfying to a goalie than a 1–0 victory for his team. And to do it in a championship game would be a dream come true.

But the Flyers weren't going to make it easy.

Ramon led a charge, dribbling the ball across the center line into Lightning territory, flanked by his teammates, Steve and Andy. There were fifty-five seconds remaining.

Ramon, Steve, and Andy set up a triangle pattern just outside the Lightning's penalty area. They passed the ball again and again, crisscrossing the three points of the triangle. With each pass, Ernie shifted his position, desperately hoping to stop the final shot attempt, hoping against hope for the 1–0 shutout.

Steve unleashed a powerful kick from the center of the field. Ernie jumped straight up and caught the ball with two hands. He landed and tossed it out to Vicki, who appeared to be open. But the Flyers' Andy sped in quickly and took control of the ball.

Thirty seconds remained.

Andy wasted no time, sending a speeding shot toward the goal. Ernie saw that he would not get to the ball in time if he tried to extend his upper body. Instead, he went into a baseball-style, feet-first slide across the front of the goal. His right foot caught a piece of the ball just before it crossed the line.

But Ramon was right there waiting.

Ernie scrambled back to get ready for the

next shot. But Ramon was too quick. With ten seconds left, Ramon launched a shot at the open part of the goal.

Ernie knew that getting back up to his feet would be a waste of precious time. From a half-crouch, half-crawling position, he flung his body across the goal in a desperate attempt at the save. If he missed, the game was tied. And that meant overtime.

Please, no overtime! was all Ernie could think as the ball sailed past his outstretched front arm.

Ernie felt a jolt to his forehead. *What was*

that? he wondered. He hit the ground and rolled up to his feet.

Time had run out, but the game was now tied. Or was it?

Ernie spun around and looked into the goal. No ball. When he turned back he saw a wave of bodies rushing right at him—his teammates! They grabbed him in a huge group hug and began jumping up and down.

That's when Ernie spotted the ball, rolling slowly to a stop, ten yards away from the goal.

"That's using your head, Big E!" Joey shouted.

Ernie started to laugh. He had just made the biggest save of his life with his head.

"Talk about a heads-up play," Ramon said, offering his hand to Ernie. "Good game, guys. We'll get you next time."

All the players who had taken part in the tournament gathered around the Lightning.

The tournament had been a huge success, thanks to Dmitri and his friends.

"Good game, guys!" said Billy Connors as he and his Stinger teammates came over to the celebrating kids. "I had a ball watching someone else play for a change."

"I had a ball, too," Ernie said. "It bounced right off my head."

Billy and the others cracked up. "Here's a little something from the Stingers," Billy said. He reached into his pocket and pulled out a thick stack of tickets. "I brought a bunch of tickets for our next home game at Rogers Stadium. There's enough here for everyone who played in the tournament. So you can come watch us play."

"Thanks, Billy!" Dmitri said.

"Good stuff!" Ernie cried. "I can't wait to watch you play, Billy. But, one thing—do you think you can get your field to look as good as ours?"